Book 6

Dedicated to my six grandchildren, the "cousins," especially to Bethany, for whom I began this journey with the "Story Girl" on "The Golden Road," six years ago. I pray all of you will find these stories about the King cousins a wonderful example for you to follow in holiness, purity, and real fun—and help you along your own journey to the heart of God.

From the author of Anne of Green Gables

L.M. Montgomery

The Story Girl
Book 6

WEDDING WISHES AND WOES

Adapted by Barbara Davoll

zonder**kidz**

zonder**kidz**.
The children's group of Zondervan

www.zonderkidz.com

Wedding Wishes and Woes
Copyright © 2005 The Zondervan Corporation, David Macdonald, trustee
and Ruth Macdonald

Requests for information should be addressed to:
Grand Rapids, Michigan 49530

Library of Congress Cataloging-in-Publication Data

Davoll, Barbara.
  Wedding wishes and woes / adaptation written by Barbara Davoll.– 1st ed.
    p. cm.
  "Adapted from The Golden Road by L. M. Montgomery."
  Summary: On Prince Edward Island, the King cousins pray for a lost cat, go
on a mayflower picnic, celebrate the conversion of Peter's father, prepare for
Aunt Olivia's wedding, and enjoy more enchanting tales from the Story Girl.
  ISBN 10: 0-310-70860-5 (softcover); ISBN 13: 978-0-310-70860-5
  [1. Storytellers — Fiction. 2. Cousins — Fiction. 3. Conduct of life — Fiction.
4. Prince Edward Island — Fiction. 5. Canada — Fiction.] I. Montgomery, L.
M. (Lucy Maud), 1874-1942. Golden road. II. Title.
  PZ7.D3216We 2005
  [Fic]–dc22

                                                      2003027957

Photograph of L. M. Montgomery used by permission of L. M. Montgomery
Collection, Archival and Special Collections, University of Guelph Library.

Zonderkidz is a trademark of Zondervan

Editor: Amy DeVries
Interior design: Susan Ambs
Art direction: Merit Alderink
Cover illustrations: Jim Griffin

Printed in the United States of America

05 06 07 08 /OPM/ 10 9 8 7 6 5 4 3 2 1

Contents

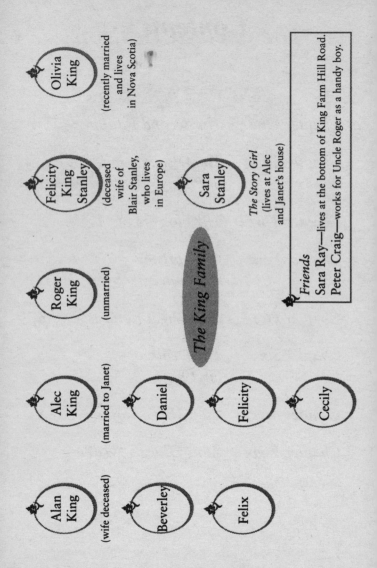

The King Family

Olivia King (recently married and lives in Nova Scotia)

Felicity King Stanley (deceased wife of Blair Stanley, who lives in Europe)

Roger King (unmarried)

Alec King (married to Janet)

Alan King (wife deceased)

Sara Stanley
The Story Girl
(lives at Alec and Janet's house)

Daniel

Felicity

Cecily

Beverley

Felix

Friends
Sara Ray—lives at the bottom of King Farm Hill Road.
Peter Craig—works for Uncle Roger as a handy boy.

The Second Edition

Miss Alice Reade is a very pretty girl. She has kind of curly blackish hair and big gray eyes and a pale face. She is tall and thin, but her figure is pretty fair. She has a nice mouth and a sweet way of speaking.

Chapter One

What a winter we had that year on Prince Edward Island. Our last adventure— being lost in a blizzard and rescued by an old woman named Peg Bowen—was thrilling enough to last a lifetime. We were now content to settle down by our fireside and work on the second edition of the newspaper we were writing, *Our Magazine*.

If you read book five, *Winter on the Island*, you'll remember that each of us made several New Year's resolutions on New Year's Day. The resolutions were not easy to keep. By February, we had a good idea who would keep their resolutions and who would not. As managing editor of our newspaper, I, Bev (please remember I am not a girl, no matter what you think of my name), decided it would be good to give credit where credit was due. I did so by printing the Resolution Honor Roll in the February edition of *Our Magazine*.

Resolution Honor Roll
Miss Felicity King

Honorable Mention
Mr. Felix King
Mr. Peter Craig
Miss Sara Ray

When the cousins saw the Resolution Honor Roll, there was quite a discussion about it all.

"I don't think it's fair that Felicity should be the only one on the Honor Roll," said Cecily, the morning the February edition of *Our Magazine* was ready.

"I don't either," agreed Peter Craig, who was our uncle Roger's handy boy.

"What do *you* have to say about it?" said Felicity hatefully. "You aren't even a member of our family."

"That doesn't matter at all," reminded our cousin Dan King. "We have all agreed that Peter and Sara Ray can be a part of the King cousins' clan, which entitles them to all rights and privileges, the same as our family."

"I knew there would be a fracas about it all," I said, "but Felicity is the only one who kept her resolution. She says she has thought a beautiful thought every morning before breakfast without missing one morning. That was the one resolution she made."

"How could she think a beautiful thought each morning?" asked the Story Girl. "I'm sure she didn't think a beautiful thought when we were at Peg Bowen's house."

"I did too," insisted Felicity. "I thought how pleasant it would be to get home and away from that weird old woman."

Felicity and the Story Girl were referring to the day we got caught in a terrible blizzard coming home from Cousin Mattie's house. It got dark and we nearly lost our lives in the blinding snowstorm. We took shelter at Peg Bowen's house. She was an old woman who some people thought was crazy and touched in the head.

"How Felicity could ever think a beautiful thought *there* is beyond me," the Story Girl said. "However, since Felicity only thinks about herself all the time, I guess it's possible."

"To make the resolution contest more fair, I have decided to give honorable mention to everybody who has kept at least one resolution perfectly," I explained. "I only wanted to give credit where credit was due. I hate to admit it, but Felicity was the only one who kept her resolution. The other three were honorable mentions."

I'm sorry, dear reader, that you have had to begin this adventure with us King cousins on such a sour note. Usually things are a bit more pleasant, and we do get along fairly well together. I guess things were a bit tense that morning. Let me introduce us to you.

As I said before, I am Bev King, the eldest of the King cousins and the brother of Felix. We are from Toronto, and have come to live for a year with our uncle Alec and aunt Janet and their three children, Felicity, Dan, and Cecily. We are staying with them on the old King farm while our father is getting established in his new job in South America. Next year we will join him there.

The old King farm is next door to another family of Kings. That is Uncle Roger and his sister, Aunt Olivia, who is his housekeeper. Sara Stanley, another cousin, whom we call the Story Girl, lives next door with Uncle Roger and Aunt Olivia. We call her the Story Girl because she tells the most wonderful stories. Like us, Sara Stanley's mother died when Sara was just a baby. We have a real bond with her because our backgrounds are similar. Her father is an artist and makes his living in Paris, France. Uncle Roger and Aunt Olivia are the guardians for the Story Girl.

Also living next door with them is Peter Craig, Uncle Roger's handy boy. He is no relation to us, but very much a part of all of us as a great friend. Another friend is Sara Ray, a neighbor girl who lives at the bottom of the King Farm Hill Road. Although

Sara Ray and Peter are not our cousins, they are almost like family to us.

This week we had a bad thing happen. Last Saturday afternoon our grown-ups gave us permission to go sledding on Uncle Roger's hill. Peter Craig and Sara Ray went along with us as well as another friend, Kitty Marr.

Aunt Olivia made sandwiches and hot chocolate for us, and Uncle Roger built a nice fire down by the pond because it was awful cold. After we ate, we began sledding. It was almost the most fun I've ever had. The hill was as fast as greased lightning. If we'd known all that was going to happen though, we might not have gone. The first thing that happened was that our cousin Dan nearly got killed.

Cecily and Sara Ray were on the sled, going down the hill, but somehow they steered wrong and went into a big snowdrift halfway down. Dan ran down to shove them out. When they started going again, he stood there for a minute just watching them. He had his back turned to us at the top of the hill, and he failed to hear Peter and the Story Girl screaming for him to get out of the way. Once they had shoved off, there was no way for them to stop.

They came racing down the hill and hit Dan from behind. Dan was thrown to the side in a crumpled heap. Peter and the Story Girl were shook up, but

Dan was so still we thought he was dead. I was the first to get to him. He was unconscious and as white as death. I stood over him, and I don't mind telling you that I was scared. Tears were coming down my face, and I was praying, "Oh, Lord, please don't let him die."

In a minute or two he groaned, and I knew he was at least alive. Uncle Roger and Aunt Olivia came running to take him up the hill to their house. His nose was bleeding, but otherwise he seemed all right. Kitty Marr was crying her head off. There was no doubt in my mind that she liked Dan, although none of us knew it before. She knelt beside Dan and wiped his face and bloody nose with her handkerchief that she had moistened in the snow.

We all breathed a sigh of relief when we saw he was all right. Dan told me later that it was worth getting hit because Kitty was so sweet to him. She told me she hadn't gotten her hanky back from him, but she didn't care. I think they are really sweet on each other, and it's fun to watch. He told me he would never again stand around in the sledding track watching girls. Now he just watches them from the sidelines.

We continued sledding, but it wasn't as much fun because Dan wasn't there the rest of the day. He is always so jolly and lots of fun. Finally the girls got tired of trudging up the hill, and they started skating down at one end of the pond. We boys continued sledding, coasting smoothly across the ice.

I don't know how it happened, but about an hour after Dan's accident, we heard the girls screaming. Somehow they had broken through the ice. Cecily was the only one who fell in, but she went in all the way. There was no danger of her drowning, but she was thoroughly drenched in the icy water.

Felix was the hero of the day. He immediately jumped on his sled, coasted down the hill and part of the way out to her. I thought he was very brave to walk out on the ice the rest of the way and pull her out, especially since he's so heavy. The ice broke under him, and he fell in too and got wet to his waist. Cecily is his favorite cousin, and you could sure tell how scared he was. He was white as a sheet as he pulled her out.

The rest of us had gotten there by then. We all took off our coats and piled them on top of Cecily like blankets. Then we ran along beside the sled as Felix pulled her up the hill to the house. She was shaking so hard that she could hardly stay on the sled, and Felix was numb with cold.

As soon as we got home, Aunt Janet and Uncle Alec took over getting them warmed up with dry clothing and hot cider. They wrapped both of them in warm blankets and made them sit close to the fire to drink their cider.

The rest of us wanted to go back to the hill for more sledding, but somehow the day was spoiled for us. It was getting dark, and Aunt Janet decided we should call it a day.

Cecily has never been very well since we got caught in the blizzard. After falling through the ice, she caught a terrible cold. We hope it doesn't develop into "newmonya."

We all remind her constantly to wear her boots and bundle up when she goes outside, but it's too late now. The damage has already been done. It's "snow wonder" she's sick again, but she really worries us. One of Uncle Alec's sisters, the Story Girl's mother, died very young with consumption. That's weak lungs, you know. Uncle Alec often says that Cecily reminds him of her. The older you get, it seems you have more and more worries.

Cecily has really been working hard to get names for her missionary quilt this year. People sign up to have their names embroidered on the big quilt they will hang at the church. They pay a nickel a name, or a dime if they want it embroidered in the corners or the center. The money will help the missionaries. Cecily has the most so far of everybody and will probably win the contest. The winner will get a whole dollar, but Cece says she will give that money to the missionaries too, if she wins.

The three most important names Cecily got for her quilt squares are the governor and his wife and Peg Bowen. Although Cecily got her name, I'm not sure she'll ever get the money from Peg Bowen. Peg ordered the most expensive location for her name—one that cost a whole dime. If she pays up, Cecily may win for getting the most subscriptions and names for the missionaries. She has done a good work in raising money for the missions. She will try to get a few more names just in case Peg doesn't pay up. Good job, Cecily!

A new boy is coming to school. His name is Cyrus Brisk, and his folks moved up from Markdale. He says he is going to punch Will Fraser's head if Willy keeps on thinking he is Cecily King's boyfriend. Cece says she doesn't have a boyfriend and probably won't for eight years. Ha!

Miss Alice Reade of Charlottetown royalty has come to Carlisle to teach music. She boards at Mr. Peter Armstrong's house. The girls are all going to take piano lessons from her. Miss Alice Reade is a very pretty girl. She has kind of curly blackish hair and big gray eyes and a pale face. She is tall and thin, but her figure is pretty fair. She has a nice mouth and a sweet way of speaking. The girls are crazy about her and talk about her all the time.

"Beautiful Alice" is what the girls call Miss Reade among themselves. They say she is divinely beautiful and that her black hair "flows back in beautiful waves from her sun-kissed brow." At least that's the way Felicity puts it. Dan says Miss Reade is really just sunburned—not "sun kissed." But that's not the same thing at all.

Personally, I think she is gorgeous. I wish I were a little older. I could go for her quite easily. Uncle Roger says she is skinny and "doesn't show her feed much." Anyway, the girls all want to be like her. I don't think they could have a much better model.

The girls are always getting up some new fad among them. They now think it is stylish to have hair ribbons to match their dresses. I guess it is also supposed to be stylish for the girls to pin a piece of ribbon on their coat that's the same color as a ribbon that a friend wears in her hair. Felicity saw that done in town and started the girls doing it here. The Story Girl thinks it's silly and so do we fellows. Girls can be so dumb sometimes, but they are pretty nice usually.

Our apples are not keeping well this year. Some of them are rotting. Uncle Alec says we are eating too many of them. We think that is better than letting them rot. Felicity and Aunt Janet will be making their applesauce and apple butter soon. This will use up a lot of the apples that we would be eating. It will keep Felix from eating them. If not, he will have to get new pants soon.

Yesterday Felicity made the best apple dumplings you ever put in your mouth. That girl can cook like a dream, and she looks so beautiful in the kitchen when her cheeks are all rosy from the heat of the oven. She had on a pretty little white apron with ruffles, and looked so delicious you could just eat her up. But let me tell you what she did. I was bragging on her dumplings to Aunt Olivia.

"I'll ask her for that recipe so Roger, Sara, and Peter can enjoy them too," Aunt Olivia said. What do you think that silly snob, Felicity, did? She *refused*— yes, you heard right—*she refused* to give Aunt Olivia the recipe.

"I'd love to give it to you, Aunt Olivia," she simpered in her sickeningly sweet voice. "But there is a real knack for doing them right. I wouldn't want you to get disappointed when you fail." Can you believe she would say that to her aunt? Why Aunt Olivia has forgotten more about cooking than she'll ever know. What a snob she is, even though she's beautiful.

Sometimes we cousins can't stand her, although Peter Craig is pretty gone on her now. He just overlooks her nasty spirit. I hope he knows what she's really like. I don't think much can be done about it. She's just what she is, and I don't think she'll ever change. Watch out, Peter. The love bug's sting is awful bad sometimes. I hope you get away from her before you get caught!

The Disappearance of Paddy

Our Paddy—the Story Girl's cat—simply disappeared. He was nowhere. One night he lapped his new milk as usual and sat on his favorite flat stone in front of the barn licking his fur clean. The next morning he was gone.

Chapter Two

Spring came late that year. It was May before the weather began to satisfy the grown-ups. But we children were more easily pleased. We thought April a splendid month because all the snow went away early and left gray, firm, frozen ground for our games. As the days slipped by, the hillsides began to look as if they were thinking of mayflowers. The old orchard was waking up and getting ready for the luscious blossoms that would turn into mouthwatering fruit.

The sky had delicate drifts of clouds as fine and filmy as a bridal veil. In the evenings, a full low moon looked over the valleys. Sounds of laughter and dreams were on the wind. The world was young again with April breezes.

"It's so nice to be alive in the spring," said the Story Girl one twilight as we swung on the low branches of the apple trees on Uncle Stephen's walk. His "walk" was a wide path in the orchard where the trees were planted as a memorial to our uncle.

He had died as a young seaman on the ocean when his vessel crashed on the rocks in a storm.

"It's nice to be alive anytime," said Felicity.

"But it's nicer in the spring," insisted the Story Girl. "When I'm dead, I think I'll *feel* dead all the rest of the year. But when spring comes, I'm sure I'll feel like getting up and being alive again."

"We've all got to die sometime," remarked Sara Ray. Her remark wasn't sad or gloomy. It was almost as if she looked forward to another world. As if she thought that her harsh mother and her own colorless personality couldn't keep her from being a star performer in heaven.

"You say the weirdest things," complained Felicity. "You won't be really dead anytime. You'll be in the next world. And I think it's horrid to talk about people being dead anyhow."

"We've all got to die," remarked Sara Ray again.

"I don't think it's so bad to think about it," commented the Story Girl. "We will spend a lot of time in heaven. Seems to me it's a good idea to think about it and make sure we are ready for it."

"I sometimes think," said Cecily, rather wearily, "that it isn't so dreadful to die young as I used to suppose." She said this with a little cough, which we were all used to by now. She had never recovered from the chill and awful cold that she had caught the night of the snowstorm, and the fall through the ice had only made it worse. There was always a black cloud of thought hanging over Cecily that maybe she was much sicker than any of us knew.

"I'm sure the next world is very beautiful, and it's nice to think about. That is, if you're sure you're going to heaven," Cecily said wistfully.

"Well, how can anyone be sure about that?" snapped Felicity.

"My aunt Jane said you can be sure by studying the Bible and doing what it says," asserted Peter.

"That's good to know, Peter. It makes me want to know more about heaven and how to get there," said Cecily.

"Let's not talk about all that dreary stuff," snapped Felicity. "Cecily, are you sure your feet aren't damp? We ought to go in anyhow. It's too chilly out here for you."

"You girls had better go," said Dan, "but I ain't going in just yet. It's not even dark."

Felicity and Cecily headed for the house while the Story Girl walked Sara Ray down the hill to her home. They had plenty of time to enjoy the walk in the spring twilight. After a while, Peter started for home, but he beckoned for me to follow. When we got behind the barn, he whispered that he needed some advice.

"You know Felicity has a birthday next week," he said, "and I want to write her an ode."

"A—a what?" I gasped.

"An ode. It's poetry, you know. I'll put it in *Our Magazine*."

"But you can't write poetry, Peter," I protested.

"I'm going to try," said Peter with determination. "I am the poetry editor, ain't I?"

"Well, yes," I admitted.

"I just wanted to know if you think she will be offended at me."

"She ought to feel flattered," I responded.

"You never can tell how she'll take things," he said gloomily. "Of course, I won't sign my name, and if she doesn't like it I won't let on that I wrote it. Don't you tell either," he warned.

I promised I wouldn't tell, and Peter went off with a happy heart. He said he meant to write two lines every day till he got it done. There was no doubt— Peter was "gone" over Felicity. He was silly in love with her.

Cupid was playing his old tricks with others that spring as well. Poor Willy Fraser was having a rough time with his heartthrob, Cecily. Although Cecily didn't care for Willy at all, she had another problem. The new kid, Cyrus Brisk, had also fallen madly in love with her. It annoyed her to be teased about

Cyrus. She had been as nasty to him as Cecily could ever be, but Cyrus was not easily discouraged.

He placed spruce gum, molasses taffy, little candy hearts, and decorated pencils on her desk at school. He chose her for all the school games, and begged her to allow him to carry her books. He even offered to work her arithmetic problems for her. It was heard that he was going to ask to walk her home some night after prayer meeting.

Cecily was disgusted and afraid that he would. She told me she would rather die than to walk home with him. But she also said she would never have the nerve to turn him down if he did ask. So far he hadn't asked—nor had he beat up on Willy Fraser as he said he would if Willy tried to cut him out with Cecily. Willy was pretty upset over the whole thing, and moped around with his face lower than a snake's belly. What was the worst for Cecily was that she could feel Cyrus staring at her all the time. She said she could just feel his loony eyes boring into her from his seat across the aisle.

And now Cyrus had written Cecily a letter—*a perfumed love letter*. He had actually sent it through the post office. Dan had picked it up and recognized the writing immediately. You could smell it from clear across the room. Did it ever stink! He must have bought the perfume from some cheap store somewhere. Dan gave Cecily no peace until she showed it to us. It was a terrible letter, poorly written with many misspellings. He signed it "Your troo luver." We laughed our heads off at it.

Felix, who was always Cecily's good friend and champion, said he would like to kick Cyrus. "He's not good enough to polish her shoes," grumped Felix. "He'd better learn to spell before he writes any more love letters."

In the letter, Cyrus said he couldn't eat or sleep for thinking of Cecily. "Maybe he'll starve to death," said Sara Ray hopefully.

"I hope he will," said Cecily cruelly. That was a lot for our mild-mannered cousin to say. "I don't plan to answer it," she asserted.

Even though she didn't answer the letter, she didn't tear it up either. After all, it was her first love letter. As a young lady twelve years of age, she was excited to receive one. Many older girls never had. It was interesting to watch. Cecily was so tender-hearted that she couldn't bear to kill an insect or hear our pigs squeal during butchering season. But the day after she received the love letter, she walked past Cyrus at school as though he weren't there. She didn't have a bit of pity for him.

It didn't matter at all to her that some of the other girls at school liked Cyrus. He sent another letter to her the next week and addressed it to "Mrs. Cecily Brisk." She was so hopping mad she could hardly see straight.

The Cupid season faded abruptly one morning. We had other important things to think about. Our Paddy—the Story Girl's cat—simply disappeared. He was nowhere. One night he lapped his new milk as usual and sat on his favorite flat stone in front of the barn licking his fur clean. The next morning he was gone. For almost a month, life was grim in the lives of the King cousins and friends.

We searched night and day for him. The Story Girl actually lost weight, and her eyes had no sparkle. And there were no stories on her heart or mind. We searched every farm, every nook and cranny, and every outbuilding on both of the King farms. We combed all the meadows and waded in all the creeks, calling his name. We drove Aunt Janet batty. She finally told us we were making fools of ourselves and begged us to quit.

"He's dead," Sara said sadly. "I just know it. He's never been gone for three days even, and now it's been three weeks. He's been poisoned—or a dog has killed him." We had just returned from Andrew Cowan's farm where a strange gray cat had been seen. The poor ugly cat was a pitiful creature with no tail. It had no likeness at all to our beautiful

Paddy with his lovely tail. There was no hope left in us. Patrick Grayfur, Esq., was no more.

Cecily said she couldn't sleep at night for dreaming about poor Paddy dying in some miserable corner where he had been mangled by a stray dog. We hated every dog we saw, thinking perhaps it might be the guilty one.

It was just the second time I had seen Sara Stanley cry. She had cried when Peter lay near death with the measles, and now she laid her head on the kitchen table and sobbed and sobbed. "It's the suspense that's so hard," she said. "If I only knew whether he's dead or alive. I just keep hoping, and that is so awful."

"Isn't that the Awkward Man coming up the lane?" asked Peter, shading his eyes from the sun.

"I believe it is," answered the Story Girl. "Wonder what brings him over here? He doesn't go out much."

As he came through the gate, he nodded to us and took off his hat. "Good evening, young folk." He was smiling and had no trace of awkwardness or shyness, which often seemed to be his way.

"Have you little people lost a cat lately?" he asked.

"Oh, yes, sir, we have," said Cecily tearfully, jumping up with hope and excitement.

Peter said, "I knew it!" in a triumphant way.

"Can you tell us anything about Paddy, Mr. Dale?" asked the Story Girl fearfully. "We have just been praying about him. He's been gone almost a month."

"Is he a silver gray cat with black points and very fine markings?"

"Yes! Yes!" we shouted.

"Well, he is over at my home, the Golden Milestone."

"Alive?"

"Yes, but very weak. You'd better come right away and make sure he is your cat," he advised. "He's pretty thin, but I think he'll pull through. I'll tell you how I found him as we go."

A joyful procession followed the Awkward Man and the Story Girl across the meadows to his home. "You know that old barn of mine back in the woods?" asked the Awkward Man. "This morning I went to the barn to move things around to put some hay in there. There had been an old upside-down barrel up on a block of wood in the barn. The barrel had been knocked down on the floor. When I moved the barrel, there was a poor little kitty under it. At first I thought he was dead. I have no idea how he got there, unless he crawled under the block and knocked it down on himself—but there he was. He was too weak to stand, so I carried him into my kitchen and gave him some milk on my finger, which he licked. I gave him milk several more times before I came for you."

"Do you suppose anyone put him under that barrel?" asked the Story Girl.

"No," answered the Awkward Man. "The barn was locked. Nothing but a cat could get in. I suppose he went under the barrel that was up on the block, perhaps trying to catch a mouse. Somehow he must have knocked the barrel over and down on himself."

By this time we had reached the Awkward Man's clean, bare kitchen, and there was our Paddy, sitting in front of his fireplace. Thin! Why he was literally skin and bone. His fur was dull and lusterless, and his tail had lost its beauty. When Sara bent down to stroke him, he gave a mournful mew and put out his little pink tongue to give her a lick. It nearly broke our hearts to see our beautiful Paddy brought so low.

"Oh, how he must have suffered," moaned Cecily.

"He'll be good as new in a week or two," the Awkward Man promised. The Story Girl gathered the cat up in her arms with a warm towel, which Mr. Dale supplied. As we started for home, Paddy snuggled into her arms with a weak little purr.

"We are so grateful, Mr. Dale," said the Story Girl as we started out the door. "You were truly an answer to prayer this morning," she stated. The precious kitty mewed pitifully, as though to thank him.

We couldn't have been happier as we carried our Paddy home. He was going back to his old familiar orchard, barn, and daily rations of new milk and cream. He would be stroked, loved, and allowed to snooze comfortably beside the fireplace. Oh, how thankful we were.

The Flowers of May

*The next day, we followed the dancing winds
to a small hill where the sunshine had got in
but never got out. In other words, it seemed
that the sun would shine forever in that place.*

Chapter Three

Words can't really describe the happiness we felt at having our Paddy back. Life was sweet, especially in the evenings. After finishing our chores, we would gather on the back step, petting and stroking him. His gentle purr and the lick of his rough little pink tongue were all we needed to make our days complete—especially so as the warmth of spring was gradually coming to the island.

"I hear that the woods are full of mayflowers now," said the Story Girl. "Why don't we have a mayflower picnic tomorrow to celebrate Paddy's safe return?"

"What's a mayflower picnic?" I asked. My brother, Felix, and I were still learning about customs on Prince Edward Island.

"I've never even heard of mayflowers in Toronto," added Felix.

"Oh, they are the most darling little flowers," said Cecily, clasping her hands together at the thought of them. There are just thousands of them, but they hide well. They grow close to rocks and hide in the grasses and under leaves. It's a lot of fun to search for them. We carry along a picnic when we go out to pick them."

"Do *boys* go along on this—picnic?" I asked doubtfully. I had never heard of boys who wanted to pick flowers.

"Sure we go," answered Peter. "It's lots of fun. We always go, don't we, Dan?"

Even Dan, who was as far away as you could get from being a sissy, agreed. "You bet! And the eats are great. Mom always packs us a wonderful picnic lunch!"

The next day, we followed the dancing winds to a small hill where the sunshine had got in but never got out. In other words, it seemed that the sun would shine forever in that place. "Let's have a contest to see who can gather the most mayflowers," suggested Felicity. It was so nice seeing her interested in something besides herself.

"I found one," squealed Cecily, excited to be the first one to find the little flower. Although the woods were full of the little clusters of star white and dawn pink flowers, they were not easy to find because they were so small. It was a real challenge to find them, but once found, we eagerly filled our baskets with the sweet-smelling little treasures. We wandered happily over the hill, sometimes following paths that separated us. We had fun calling to one another to come see our lovely harvest.

When the sun began to hang low in the sky, we all got hungry. We found a shallow pool in the meadow and ate our picnic along its ferny banks. Aunt Janet had outdone herself, filling our basket with tiny sandwiches and little cakes iced with frosting. We washed them down with cool tea and sat talking about the beauty around us. I was glad we boys had been included. Then we stripped our flowers of any faded leaves and stems and made up bouquets to take home to our aunts and uncles and parents.

While we made up the bouquets, the Story Girl told us the story of a beautiful Indian maiden who had died of a broken heart when the first snows of winter fell. Her true lover had been unable to return because of the deep snows, but she believed that his absence meant he had been untrue.

When he returned and found her dead, he went to mourn at her grave. It was there that he found the sweet sprays of a flower he'd never seen before. They seemed to be a message of love and remembrance from his dark-eyed sweetheart. "And that is how the first mayflowers were found," said the Story Girl, finishing her tale.

"Is there anything else to eat in the basket?" asked Dan.

"Dan, don't be such a pig," said Felicity. "You're gross and not a bit refined," she said, watching him carve up the piece of ham with his pocketknife and eat it noisily.

"You're right, my love," he said sarcastically. "I am a pig, I'm afraid. But then that makes you a pig's sister, darling."

Felicity tossed her beautiful head in disgust.

"I like bacon, but I can never look at a pig without wondering whether we should eat it or not," said Cecily. "The Jews were not supposed to eat pork, you know."

"Well, I'm glad I don't have to worry about it. I sure do like any kind of pork as well as anything I know," said Dan, licking his fingers for the last bit of taste.

When we finished our lunch, the woods were already wrapping themselves in the dim, blue dusk of twilight. Out in the meadows, there was enough light for us to see, and the robins happily whistled us home. As we crossed the green pastures, we could see the pale yellow outline of a new moon. It had been such a splendid day for all of us.

Upon reaching home, we found that the famous Miss Reade (Beautiful Alice) had been visiting our home on the hill and was just leaving. The Story Girl went for a walk with her and came back with an important expression on her face.

"You look as if you have a story to tell," said Felix.

"One is growing. It isn't a whole story yet," answered the Story Girl mysteriously.

"What is it?" asked Cecily. "Is it about the Awkward Man?"

"I can't tell you until it's fully grown," said the Story Girl. "But tonight I'll tell you a pretty little story the Awkward Man told us—told me. It's a fairy story but, oh, so sweet. . . .

"He was walking in his garden as we went by his house. We were looking at his tulip beds. His tulips are up ever so much higher than ours. I asked him how he managed to coax them along so early. He said *he* didn't do it—it was all the work of the pixies who live in the woods across the brook."

"Pixies are little fairies, you know," stated Sara, seeing the questions on our faces.

"He said there were more pixie babies than usual this spring, and the mothers were in a hurry for the cradles. The tulips are the pixie babies' cradles, it seems.

"The mother pixies come out of the woods at twilight and rock their tiny little brown babies to sleep in the tulip cups. This is the reason why tulip blooms last so much longer than other blossoms. The pixie babies must have a cradle until they are grown up. They grow very fast, you see, and the

41

Awkward Man says on a spring evening when the tulips are out, you can hear the sweetest, softest, clearest, fairy music in his garden. It is the pixie folk singing as they rock the pixie babies to sleep."

"Nonsense!" said Felicity. "We all know there is no such thing as fairy babies. I've never seen one. Have you?" she sneered.

"No, I haven't," admitted our Story Girl. "But I would like to. The Awkward Man says you must have a good imagination to hear them. And, Felicity, I'm afraid you have none. Now, if you'll excuse me, I'm going out to hear the pixies sing their babies to sleep."

"May I come too?" asked Cecily. "I promise to bring my imagination."

Felicity flounced out of the room and up to bed. "Enjoy yourself," she snipped. "I would far rather be of a practical nature."

"Of course, beloved," said Dan sarcastically, bowing to her as she went by him.

When they stepped out of the house, Cecily walked softly along the walk, listening eagerly for the pixie mother's lullabies. "Listen, Sara. I think I hear them singing," she said. The girls stood, scarcely breathing, straining their ears to hear. The sounds of twilight swept around them. Little crickets and katydids called to each other. From down in the meadow, the frogs called good night, and tiny fireflies flitted about as if to light the pixies' way to the little tulip cradles.

"Oh, what a dear thought," whispered Cecily. She stooped and gently rocked a lovely yellow tulip cradle. "I will never see tulips again that I don't think of the little pixies singing to their babies. Please thank the Awkward Man for that story, Sara. He has a wonderful imagination for a man. I wonder if he will ever marry and rock his own little ones to sleep?"

The Story Girl smiled as if she knew some lovely secret. She stood drinking in the sights and sounds around her.

"You will be the first one I'll tell if I ever find out the answer to that question, Cece. Oh, this beauty is more than I can bear tonight," Sara Stanley said, spreading her arms as if to hug the night.

Above them the heavens were a carpet of stars winkling at them. Just to the left of the old King farmhouse, there was a glorious display as a falling star sped downward toward earth.

"Maybe that star is carrying a pixie father," said Cecily softly. "Perhaps he is coming to tell his tiny children a bedtime story."

Sara linked her arm with Cecily's, and they walked dreamily toward the house. Inside the King's brightly lit kitchen, there was a cozy fire. They could hear their cousins laughing as they played a game.

Life was good, and they were happy to have each other and their family. Cecily blew a soft kiss to the imaginary pixies. "Sleep tight, babies," she called as they stepped into the house.

A Surprising Announcement

"It was interesting when Paddy was gone,"
said the Story Girl thoughtfully. "Although
we suffered a lot when he was lost, I still
believe I'd rather be miserable than dull."

Chapter Four

Spring on the King's farm was a blush of wonder, as it seemed the whole world was alive and greening. Late one May evening, we were sitting enjoying the wonderful smells coming from the orchard. A hedge of lilacs grew directly behind a long row of blossoming cherry trees. When the breezes blew, there was no sweeter fragrance on earth.

It should have been enough just to be alive and young in that wondrous place, but Sara Stanley was restless. "Nothing exciting has happened for ever so long," said the Story Girl with a pout.

"I don't like excitement very much," said Cecily. "It makes me so tired. I'm sure it was exciting enough when Paddy was missing. But we didn't find it very pleasant."

"It was interesting when Paddy was gone," said the Story Girl thoughtfully. "Although we suffered a lot when he was lost, I still believe I'd rather be miserable than dull."

"I wouldn't," said Felicity decidedly.

Peter was lying on his back, looking up at the trees. "Why do you suppose that Lombardy poplar tree holds its branches straight up in the air like that when the other poplar trees hang theirs down?" he asked.

"Because it grows that way," said Felicity, giving no information at all.

"I know a story about the aspen poplar tree. Aunt Jane told me this one," Peter said.

We all sat listening. This was something different, Peter telling a story.

"Have you ever noticed that the aspen's leaves are always shaking?" he asked. We nodded. "Even when there is no wind they are always moving. Aunt Jane said it is an old legend that the cross on which the Savior of the world suffered was made of aspen poplar wood. To this day its leaves are always shivering because of the terrible thing that happened to it."

"It does look sad," said Felix, "but it is a pretty tree, and it wasn't its fault."

"This dew is getting heavy," said Felicity, interrupting our serious thoughts. "It's time for us to go in. If we don't, we'll all have a cold. Then we'll all be miserable enough, but it won't be too exciting."

"All the same, I wish something exciting would happen," said the Story Girl as we walked up through the orchard.

"You may get your wish," said Peter, "but you can never tell."

The Story Girl did get her wish. Something exciting happened the very next day.

When the Story Girl came over the next afternoon, we knew immediately that something was up. She looked as if she'd been crying, but we saw hope in her eyes.

"I have some news to tell you," she said importantly. "Can you guess what it is?"

We couldn't and wouldn't even try.

"Tell us right off," begged Felix. "You look as if it's something huge."

"It is. Aunt Olivia is going to be married."

"Aunt Olivia? I don't believe it," cried Felicity. "Who told you?"

"Aunt Olivia herself. So it is perfectly true. I'm awfully sorry in one way—because I will miss her so much. But won't it be splendid to have a real wedding in the family? She's says it will be a big wedding, and I am to be a bridesmaid."

"You're not old enough to be a bridesmaid," Felicity said spitefully.

"I'm nearly fifteen. Anyway, Aunt Olivia says I have to be."

"Who's she going to marry?" asked Cecily, gathering herself together after the shock.

"His name is Dr. Seton, and he is a man from Halifax, Nova Scotia. She met him when she was at Uncle Edward's last summer. They've been writing to each other ever since and have just become engaged. The wedding is to be the third week in June."

"And our school concert comes the next week," complained Felicity. "Why do things always come together like that? And what are you going to do if Aunt Olivia is going away?"

"I'm coming to live at your house," answered the Story Girl rather timidly. She didn't think Felicity would like it, but Felicity took it pretty well.

"You spend most of your time here anyhow, so it will just mean that you'll sleep and eat here too. But what will become of Uncle Roger? Who will keep house for him?"

"Aunt Olivia says he'll have to get married too. But Uncle Roger says he'd rather *hire* a housekeeper than *marry* one. He says if a housekeeper doesn't please him, he can fire her and get another, but not so with a wife."

"There will be a lot of cooking to do for the wedding," said Felicity in a pleased tone.

"Just think, the Story Girl will have her name in the newspaper if she's a bridesmaid," said Sara Ray in awe.

"In the Halifax papers too," added Felix, "since Dr. Seton comes from Halifax. What is his first name?"

"Robert."

"And will we have to call him Uncle Robert?"

"Not until he's married to her. Then we will, of course."

We all sat, thinking of the change that was coming to our little world. "Just think of it! Aunt Olivia gone from us. It's hard to even imagine," said Cecily. "Do you know much about our new uncle?" she asked Story Girl.

"Not much more than I have told you," answered Sara.

"Will he be a good husband for her?" asked Peter.

"Oh, yes, I think so. She says he is very kind. He is a doctor, you know. Aunt Olivia says that one day a week he leaves his practice in the city of Halifax and goes in his buggy to little surrounding villages that don't have a doctor. He doesn't charge those who are poor and takes care of folk who could not afford to pay a doctor," said Sara.

Peter was thinking of his own father who had been such a disappointment to his mother. Mr. Craig was a drunkard, and poor Mrs. Craig had to take in washings to make a living for herself and her son. Of course, now that Peter was old enough to help, he

51

was working as Uncle Roger's handy boy. Because of the trouble his family had seen, Peter was much more sensitive about marriage and family matters.

"I hope he is a good man and will treat our aunt Olivia well," said Peter.

"I feel certain that he will be, but I really don't know," said the Story Girl.

"I think we ought to find out, don't you?" asked Peter.

"I think so too," said Cecily. "We don't really know him, and he does live far away from us. I couldn't bear to think of Aunt Olivia having an unhappy home."

"Neither could I," agreed my brother, Felix.

I was thinking about our own home, and how much my father had loved my mother. We had such a happy home, and we still miss our mother terribly since she died. It has been hard for Felix and me and Father since then. We knew it was very important to find the right mate.

"Well, why don't we ask her about it. Here she comes now on her way over to see Aunt Janet," said the Story Girl.

Sure enough, Aunt Olivia was coming down the lane between our farms. She opened the gate of the picket fence and headed into the orchard toward us. We were sitting under the trees of Uncle

Stephen's walk that served as a shortcut between the two farms.

"Well, my favorite little nieces and nephews," she called happily. "Has the Story Girl told you my good news?"

We all sat staring at our favorite aunt. "My goodness, what a sad lot you are," she observed, pausing to talk. "I would think you would be jumping up to congratulate me," she laughed.

"Oh, we are very thrilled for you, Aunt Olivia, but we are so—so sad to think of losing you," said our sweet little Cecily. "We—I—we all will miss you terribly," she added, with a tearful little voice.

"Oh, my little dears," she said, stooping to scoop Cecily into her arms. "I, too, will miss you terribly. But you aren't *losing* me," she cried. "You will know exactly where I am, and you can come to visit us by ferry. Uncle Robert is terribly excited about gaining so many wonderful new family members. And we will write letters and tell you all the fun things we are doing."

"Aunt Olivia, my cousins and I are just wondering about the man you are marrying," said Sara Stanley, coming right to the point, as she usually did.

"Oh, you dears. Do you remember when your aunts and uncles went to Halifax with me last summer?" asked Aunt Olivia.

We all nodded. We would never forget the time our grown-ups had trusted Uncle Roger and us with the care of the houses and farms while they were gone.

"Well, that was when I and my brothers and sisters met him," continued Aunt Olivia. "They have all met him now. That is, all except Bev and Felix's father have met him. But we have written to Alan in South America, and he has approved of our marriage. My fiancé is well known to those of our family who live in Halifax. In fact, Robert had to receive permission from Uncle Alec, as my oldest brother, for us to marry."

"That's enough for me, Aunt Olivia," I said. "If our grown-ups all approve, we know it will be fine."

"Isn't he a lot older than you, Aunt Olivia?" questioned Cecily, still a bit doubtful.

"Well, yes, he is, Cece," laughed Aunt Olivia. "He is six years older than I, which may seem like a lot to you now. But to adults, that is not a long time at all. Because he is a doctor, his education took a long time. He is an outstanding citizen in Halifax, and has been asked to run for governor someday. You see, sometimes being older is better because you have a lot of experience and can help others."

Suddenly I felt a new responsibility as the oldest cousin. I got up and gave Aunt Olivia a hug, and each of the cousins followed. All of our hearts were a whole lot lighter as we walked into the house with her. It was such a huge moment for us.

It was the first time that our family circle was going to be changed. Who knew what else would happen? Why, maybe our old family bachelor, Uncle Roger, would get married next. I think we all felt a lot of excitement for Aunt Olivia—and for Uncle Robert. I could hardly wait to meet such a fine man.

The Story Girl had gotten her wish for sure. Something exciting was surely going to happen, and nothing would ever be the same again. It was part of our passage to growing up.

A Prodigal Returns

Peter joined us with a weird expression
on his face. He seemed bursting with some
news, which he wanted to tell and yet
hesitated to do so. "Why are you looking so
mysterious, Peter?" demanded the Story Girl.

Chapter Five

Aunt Olivia and the Story Girl lived in a whirlwind of dressmaking after the wedding was announced. The girls enjoyed it greatly. Cecily and Felicity also had to have new dresses for the event. They couldn't be bothered to talk of anything else for a month. The newspaper, *Our Magazine,* was forgotten by the girls until the wedding was over. We fellows had to get along the best we could, writing and editing it as they dreamed of new clothes and the wedding.

Cecily declared that she hated to sleep because she was sure to dream that she was at Aunt Olivia's wedding in her old faded gingham dress and a ragged apron.

"And no shoes or stockings," she added, "and I can't move. In my dream, everyone walks past and looks at my ugly feet."

"That's only in a dream," mourned Sara Ray. "But I'll probably have to wear my last summer's white dress to the wedding. It's too short, but Ma says it's plenty good for this summer. I'll just be mortified if I have to wear it."

"I'd rather not go at all than to wear a dress that wasn't proper," said Felicity in her usual proud way.

"I'd go to the wedding if I had to go in my school dress," cried Sara Ray. "I've never been to anything—not even a funeral. I wouldn't miss it for the world."

"Aunt Jane always said that if you are neat and tidy, it doesn't matter whether you're finely dressed or not," said Peter.

"I'm sick of hearing about your aunt Jane," said Felicity crossly. "She's dead!"

Peter looked grieved but held his tongue. Felicity was very nasty to him that spring, but his loyalty never wavered. Everything she said or did was right—in Peter's eyes.

"It's all very well to be neat and tidy," said Sara Ray. "But I like a little style too."

"Maybe your mother will get you a new dress after all," comforted Cecily. "Anyway, nobody will notice you because everyone will be looking at the bride. Aunt Olivia will make a lovely bride. Just think how sweet she'll look in a white silk dress and a floating veil."

"The ceremony is to be held out here in the orchard under the tree that is named for her," said the Story Girl. "Won't that be romantic? It almost makes me feel like getting married myself."

"What a way to talk," scoffed Felicity. "And you only fifteen."

"Lots of people have been married at fifteen," laughed the Story Girl. "Lady Jane Gray was."

One Saturday night, Peter's mother came by to get him for his Sunday visit. She was a plump, black-eyed little woman, neat as a pin. I think her curly-haired boy, Peter, was all that kept her heart and spirit going.

Peter went home with her, and returned Sunday evening to find us sitting in the orchard around the Pulpit Stone. We hadn't had any preaching contests yet that year, but the Pulpit Stone was a favorite spot of ours. We always learned our memory verses for Sunday school there, by saying them to each other. Paddy, the Story Girl's cat, had grown sleek and handsome again. Now he sat on the Pulpit Stone, washing his face with his little paws.

Peter joined us with a weird expression on his face. He seemed bursting with some news, which he wanted to tell and yet hesitated to do so.

"Why are you looking so mysterious, Peter?" demanded the Story Girl.

"What do you think has happened?" asked Peter seriously.

"What?" we all questioned.

"My *father* has come home," answered Peter.

His announcement stunned us.

"Peter! When?" we all shouted at once.

"Saturday night. He was there when Ma and I got home. It was a terrible shock for Ma, and I didn't even know him at first."

"Peter Craig, I believe you are glad your father has come back," cried the Story Girl.

"Of course I'm glad," agreed Peter.

"And after you said you never wanted to see him again," said Felicity.

"You just wait. You haven't heard my story yet. I wouldn't have been glad to see Father if he'd come back the same as he was when he went away. But he is a changed man. He happened to go into a revival meeting up in Maine one night this spring and got himself converted. Now he says he's come home to look after his family. He says he's never going to drink another drop ... and Ma isn't to do any more washing for nobody but us.

"And I'm not to be a hired boy any longer. He says I can stay with your uncle Roger until the fall because I promised I would, but after that I'm to stay home and go to school and learn to be whatever I'd like to be. I tell you, we didn't know what to think. Everything seemed upside down. But he gave Ma forty dollars—every cent he had. I guess he really is converted for sure."

"I hope it will last," said Felicity. She didn't say it nastily though. We were all glad for Peter's sake.

"How happy you must be," said Sara Ray in a dreamy voice. "It's so romantic."

"I think Father has been in a terrible prison," said Peter. "A prison of his own bad habit. But a power mightier than the forces of evil has freed him and led him back to liberty and to his family. I believe now that God can do anything.

"Of course, I'm awfully glad he's come back," Peter continued, "but something is worrying me. I'll miss you all terribly bad. I won't even be able to go to school with you now because we live in Markdale, and I'll have to go to school there."

"But you must come and see us often," said Felicity graciously. "Markdale isn't so far away, and you could spend every other Saturday afternoon with us anyway." The way she was looking at Peter said a lot more than her words. We saw that she really did like him.

Peter's black eyes were filled with adoration and gratitude.

"That's so kind of you, Felicity. I'll come as often as I can, of course. But it won't be the same as being around all the time. The other thing is even worse. You see, it was a Methodist revival that Father got converted in, and so, of course, he joined the Methodist church. He wasn't anything before.

"He used to say he was a 'nothing-garian,' and he lived up to it—kind of bragging like. But he's a strong Methodist now, and he's going to go to the Markdale Methodist Church and help pay the minister there. Now what will he say when I tell him I'm a Presbyterian?"

"You haven't told him yet?" asked the Story Girl.

"No, I didn't dare. I was scared he'd say that I'd have to be a Methodist."

"Well, Methodists are pretty near as good as Presbyterians," said Felicity, seeming to be very agreeable.

"I guess they're every bit as good," answered Peter. "But that ain't the point. I've got to be a Presbyterian 'cause I joined the Presbyterian church. And once I decide something, I stick to it. But I'm afraid it will make Father mad or discourage him."

"Peter, do you think it really matters?" asked the Story Girl in her reasonable way. "Think how great it would be for the three of you to go to church together. Think how that would please both your mother and father. And it will help bind your family together."

"Yes, and if you all go together now, you may come to like it best," I added. "If not, you can change to the Presbyterian church later when you grow up and move away from home."

64

Peter looked around at all of us who were more than friends. He was really part of our family. At least, that is how we thought of him.

"You know, that is right," he said. "What difference is there? What's important is that Father is a changed man, and I want to do all I can to help him. I think I'm going to go with my parents to church. I still have a lot to learn about all of this. I just can hardly believe it's all happened. Somehow it will make up for not being here all the time with you."

"We will miss you, Peter," said Felicity sweetly, tucking her arm into his and smiling up at him. We could just see Peter melt at her look. The two of them walked away toward the house, smiling and talking quietly.

"Oh, my," sighed Cecily, looking after them. "I wonder if I'll ever have a boyfriend."

"I can't help wondering too, but I know I'll never have a husband ... I just know it," Sara said, bursting into real tears.

"Well, men don't like crybabies," said Cecily wisely. Cecily had a good deal of common sense tucked away underneath her smooth brown hairdo.

"Cecily, do you ever intend to be married?" asked Sara in a confidential tone.

"Goodness!" cried Cecily, quite shocked. "There will be plenty of time to think about that when I'm grown up, Sara."

"I should think you'd have to think of it now, with Cyrus Brisk as crazy after you as he is."

"I wish Cyrus Brisk was at the bottom of the Red Sea," exclaimed Cecily. "I can't stand the mention of his name."

"What has Cyrus been doing now?" asked Story Girl, coming around the corner of the hedge.

"Doing now! It's *all* the time. He just worries me to death," moaned Cecily in anger. "He keeps writing me letters and putting them in my desk or in my reading book. I never answer any of them, but he keeps on. In the last one, he said he was going to do something desperate right off if I wouldn't promise to marry him when we grow up."

"Just think, Cecily, you've had a proposal already," said Sara Ray in an awe-struck tone.

"But he hasn't done anything desperate yet, and that was last week. He sent me a lock of his hair and wanted one of mine in exchange," scoffed Cecily. "I sent his back to him pretty quick."

"Haven't you answered any of his letters?" asked Sara Ray.

"I have not!" said Cecily firmly.

"What if you were to write him just once and tell him exactly what you think of him in good, plain English? It might cure him of his nonsense," said Sara Ray.

"I couldn't do that. I haven't the courage," Cecily confessed, with a blush. "But I'll tell you what I did do. Last week he wrote me a long letter. It was awful and every other word was spelled wrong. He even spelled baking soda 'bacon soda'!"

"What on earth had he to say about baking soda in a love letter?" asked Sara Ray.

"Oh, he said his mother sent him to the store for some, and he forgot it because he was thinking about me. Well, I just took his letter and sent it back to him. I wrote in all the words spelled right in red ink above the wrong ones, just like Mr. Perkins makes us do with our spelling lesson. I thought maybe he'd feel insulted and stop writing to me."

"And did he?"

"No, he didn't. I think you can't insult Cyrus Brisk. He's too thickheaded. He wrote another letter and thanked me for correcting his mistakes. He said it made him feel glad, because he said I was beginning to take an interest in him when I wanted him to spell better. Did you ever? My Sunday school teacher says it is wrong to hate anyone, but I don't care. I hate Cyrus Brisk."

"Mrs. Cyrus Brisk *would* be an awful name," giggled Sara Ray. "Flossie Brisk says Cyrus is ruining all the trees on his father's farm by cutting your name on them. His father told him he would whip him if he didn't stop. But Cyrus keeps right on. He told Flossie it relieved his feelings. Flossie says he cut your initials and his together on the birch tree in front of the parlor window. They had a row of hearts around them." explained Sara Ray.

"Just where every visitor can see them, I suppose," mourned Cecily. "He just worries the life out of me. And what I mind most of all is that he sits and looks at me in school with big calf eyes when he ought to be doing his math sums. Even though I don't look at him, I can *feel* him staring at me. It makes me so nervous."

"And he sends me pieces of poetry he cuts out of the newspaper," Cecily went on.

Those two silly girls read the sentimental rhyme and giggled over it. Poor Cyrus! His young love was sadly misplaced. Although Cecily never "gave in to him," he didn't condemn himself to a loveless life. Quite early in life, he married a plump, rosy girl and raised a large and respectable family. He became a justice of the peace, which was a very good job for him.

It was amazing to see the change in Peter's father. One day Felix and I went to Carlisle to buy some seeds for Uncle Alec and saw Mr. and Mrs. Craig. They were in the hardware store buying a new hoe and rake and some seeds for their garden. We hardly recognized Mrs. Craig. She had on a new hat and dress and looked almost as lovely as the governor's wife.

She had covered her raw, work-roughened hands with white kid gloves, and her eyes were sparkling. Her lined face was free from care, and her cheeks were as rosy as a new bride. Mr. Craig had trimmed his beard, and his handsome face had blue eyes that twinkled just like Peter's.

"Why, hello, boys," said Mrs. Craig, introducing us. "My dear, this is Beverly and Felix King. They are the sons of Alan King, Alec's brother, you will remember. They are staying at the King farm with Alec and Janet until their father becomes established in South America in his new position with his firm."

Mr. Craig, who was as well-dressed as a judge, put forth his hand with a smile. "Well, boys, I've heard so much about you from our son, Peter. He certainly puts great confidence in you young men. I'm so happy that Peter has had such fine friends to influence him in the right way."

I'm sure our mouths hung open in amazement. Where was the scruffy, shiftless person we had seen once before, who always had tobacco juice in his beard? Where was the drunken stumblebum with the slurred voice and unclear eyes? Could this be the same man? Indeed it was. Could his conversion to Christianity have made such a difference?

"Ho, Mother," Mr. Craig laughed in a hearty voice. "I'm sure they don't recognize me as the same drunk they've heard of before. I am a changed man, fellows. When I was not much older than you, I began the downward trail of alcohol abuse that has caused so much sorrow for my dear wife and son. Perhaps you've heard of the revival meeting where I heard that Christ was the answer. Now that I have become a Christian man, all things have become new. We hope to have the opportunity to get to know Peter's friends now that I've come home."

His little wife tucked her arm into his and looked adoringly at him. "Yes, please come over anytime," she added in her soft, cultured voice. "We are so thankful for what God has done."

"Now, if you'll excuse us," Mr. Craig said, "I've a lot of catching up to do at home. You know, things that my dear Betsy and Peter have not been able to do. I'm mending fences this afternoon and also hope to get the garden planted. So we'll say good-bye for now." And lifting his hat to them politely, the happy couple went their way.

"We're so happy for you," I stammered.

"We'll be sure to tell Peter we saw you," Felix called after them.

The little bell on the door clanged as it shut, and we were still standing where they left us. We couldn't believe what we had seen. The storekeeper gave a polite little cough, and we came to our senses, paid for our seed, and left the store.

"Felix, do you realize that we have seen the results of an absolute miracle?" I asked, as we walked down the street.

"I do, Bev. Who would ever think such a change could come about because of a decision he made? The power of God to change a life is wonderful."

"Don't ever forget it," I said in my big-brother voice. "No one can ever doubt that God is real after seeing that."

I could hardly wait to see our friend Peter and tell him what we'd seen. I would never forget it the rest of my life.

The Death of First Love

Mr. Perkins was very strict with discipline.
No talking of any kind was allowed
between pupils during school hours.
Anyone caught was promptly punished by
a variety of terrible corrections for which
Mr. Perkins was famous. Usually they
were worse than an ordinary whipping.

Chapter Six

June was crowded full of interest that year. Cecily declared she hated to go to sleep for fear she might miss something. There were so many dear delights along the Golden Road to give us pleasure. The earth was alive with summer's new blossoms. There were the dancing shadows in the fields, the rustling of the rain-wet woods. There was the fragrance of flowers in the meadow, the lilting of birds, and the drone of bees in the old orchard.

There was a sweet pain to the joyful earth around us, sunset behind the pines, dew-filled primrose cups, crescent moons peeking through the dark pine boughs, and soft nights lit with twinkling stars. We enjoyed all this beauty as children do, unthinking and with light hearts.

Besides all of this, there were the happy preparations for Aunt Olivia's mid-June wedding and the excitement of practicing for the school concert with our teacher, Mr. Perkins. The concert marked the close of our school year.

I guess the best fun was watching Cecily's troubles with Cyrus Brisk, though Cecily didn't seem to think it was funny at all. Matters went from bad to worse in regard to their love quarrel. Cyrus continued to shower Cecily with horribly spelled notes. She was sickened by his constant threats to fight Willy Fraser over her. The sad thing was that Willy Fraser could not have cared less, as Felicity, in her sarcastic manner, often pointed out. Cyrus threatened Willy, but he never followed through.

"But I'm always afraid he will," said Cecily. "It would be such a disgrace to have two boys fighting over me in school."

"You *must* have encouraged Cyrus a little in the beginning, or he'd give up," said Felicity unjustly.

"I never did!" cried Cecily in an outrage. "You know very well, Felicity King, that I have hated Cyrus Brisk ever since the day I first saw his big, fat, red face. So there!" Then as a second thought she added, "Well, maybe I don't *hate* him, but I sure have a violent dislike."

Cecily's conscience just wouldn't let her hate anybody, but her feelings were evident—she didn't care for him at all.

"Felicity is just jealous because Cyrus took a liking to you instead of her, Sis," said Dan.

"Talk sense!" snapped Felicity.

"If I did you wouldn't understand me, sweet little sister," Dan said smartly.

One sunny afternoon in school, Cecily and Kitty Marr asked and received permission to sit on the side bench by the open window, where it was coolest. To sit on this bench was always considered a treat, and Mr. Perkins only allowed it as a reward. But Cecily and Kitty had another reason for wishing to sit there. Kitty had read in a magazine that sunbaths were good for the hair. So both she and Cecily tossed their long braids over the windowsill and let them hang there in the broiling sunshine.

While Cecily diligently worked a fraction problem on her slate, Cyrus asked Mr. Perkins for permission to go out. Once outside, he sneaked up close to the window and cut off a piece of Cecily's hair.

Cyrus bragged about his accomplishment at recess, showing off the piece of braid to all the boys and causing quite an uproar. Cecily cried all the way home from school and only stopped when her brother, Dan, said he was going to fight Cyrus and make him give it up.

"Oh, no, you mustn't, Dan," sobbed Cecily, struggling to stop crying. "I won't have you fighting on my account for anything. And besides, he'll likely lick you—he's so big and rough. And the folks at home might find out all about it. Uncle Roger would never give me any peace, and Mother would be cross.

She'll never believe it wasn't my fault. It wouldn't be so bad, but he cut a great big chunk right off the end of one of my braids. I'll have to cut the other one to make them even, and they'll look so terribly stubby."

But getting the hunk of Cecily's hair was the last triumph for Cyrus. His downfall was near, although it involved Cecily in another humiliating experience. She cried for days. But in the end, she confessed it was worth going through it just to get rid of Cyrus.

It happened this way. Mr. Perkins was very strict with discipline. No talking of any kind was allowed between pupils during school hours. Anyone caught was promptly punished by a variety of terrible corrections for which Mr. Perkins was famous. Usually they were worse than an ordinary whipping.

One day in school, Cyrus sent a letter across to Cecily. Usually he left his love notes in her desk or between the leaves of her books, but this time he passed it to her under the desks and through the hands of two or three students. Just as Em Frewen held it over the aisle, Mr. Perkins wheeled around from the blackboard and caught her in the act.

"Bring that here, Emmeline," he commanded.

Cyrus turned quite pale. Em carried the note to Mr. Perkins, who took it, held it up, and looked at the address.

"Did you write this to Cecily, Emmeline?" he asked.

"No, sir."

"Then who did write it?"

Em said she didn't know—it had just been passed over from the next row.

"And I suppose you have no idea where it came from?" he said, with his frightful grin. "Well, perhaps Cecily can tell us. You may take your seat, Emmeline. You will remain last in your spelling class for a week as punishment for passing the note. Cecily, come here."

Indignant, Em sat down and poor, innocent Cecily went up with a red face.

"Cecily," said her tormentor, "do you know who wrote this letter to you?"

Cecily could not tell a lie.

"I—I think so, sir," she murmured faintly.

"Who was it?"

"I can't tell you that," stammered Cecily, who by now was on the verge of tears.

"Ah!" said Mr. Perkins politely. "Well, I suppose I could easily find out by opening it. But it is very impolite to open another person's letters. I think I have a better plan. Since you refuse to tell me who wrote it, I would like you to open the letter and copy the contents on the blackboard, where we may all read and enjoy them. Don't forget to sign the writer's name at the bottom."

"Oh," gasped Cecily, choosing to do the lesser of two evils. "I'll tell you who it was."

"Hush," said Mr. Perkins. "You did not obey when I first ordered you to tell me the name of the writer. You cannot have the privilege of doing so now. Open the letter, take the chalk, and write it on the board."

Even meek, mild, obedient little souls like Cecily may be goaded to wild rebellion.

"I—I won't," she cried passionately.

Now, Cecily was a favorite of Mr. Perkins, and he thought it was just a silly note from one of the girls. But to let her off now, when she had defied him, was unthinkable.

"So you really think you won't?" he smiled. "Well, on second thought, either do as I ask, or you will sit for three days with"—his eyes scanned the room to find a boy sitting alone—"with—Cyrus Brisk."

Now, the interesting part of this little drama was that Mr. Perkins had no idea that the note was from Cyrus, nor did he know that Cyrus liked Cecily. Although, at the time, we thought it was just sheer cruelty on his part. Either way, Cecily was left with no choice. She would have done anything to keep from sitting with Cyrus. With flashing eyes, she tore open the letter, snatched the chalk, and dashed to the blackboard.

In a few minutes, the entire contents of the letter were on the board for all to see. In his usual misspelled way, Cyrus wrote that he "wore her hare over his hart—and he stole it." He wrote that her "eyes were so sweet and lovely that he coudn't find words nice enuf to describ them," and that he "could never forget how butiful she had looked in prar meeting the evening before" and that "some meels he couldn't eat for thinking of her." He signed it, "yours til deth do us part, Cyrus Brisk."

As Cecily wrote, the classroom exploded into smothered laughter. Mr. Perkins himself could not keep a straight face. He turned abruptly away and looked out the window, but we could see his shoulders shaking. When Cecily had finished and bitterly thrown down the chalk, he turned around with a very red face.

"That will do, Cecily. You may sit down. Cyrus, since it seems you are the guilty person, take the eraser and clean the board. Then go stand in the corner, facing the room, and hold your arms straight above your head until I tell you to take them down."

Cyrus obeyed, and Cecily ran to her seat and wept. Mr. Perkins left her alone for the remainder of the day. She bore it bitterly for several days, until she was comforted by the realization that Cyrus had stopped persecuting her. He wrote no more letters, and no longer gazed at her in adoration. He didn't bring her gum or candy.

At first we thought he had been cured by the punishment, but soon his sister told Cecily the true reason. Cyrus at last had been driven to believe that Cecily really didn't like him. He figured if she hated him so intensely that she would rather write the note on the blackboard than sit with him, what use was it to continue to sigh like a furnace for her.

Mr. Perkins had ended love's young dream for Cyrus with a killing frost. And dear Cecily felt it had been worth it. She was allowed to enjoy her young life again, with no calf eyes watching her in adoration. Sweet peace at last.

Or at least for a while. Now that Cyrus Brisk was a thing of the past, Willy Fraser had become more interesting to Cecily's future. Secretly she had always liked him and had enjoyed the thought of him fighting with Cyrus over her.

"Now Willy Fraser can have his chance to be your boyfriend," sighed Sara Ray. Cecily's poor friend, Sara Ray, had never had the privilege of having a boy fighting over her. In fact, most boys in our school would have punched any fellow who accused him of liking Sara Ray.

"Oh, for pity's sake," said Cecily, answering Sara Ray. "Willy doesn't want to be my boyfriend.

He talked a lot about punching Cyrus, but he never did. If he liked me, he would have done something about it."

"If you silly girls will kiss and make up, maybe you ought to let Willy Fraser know that he has smooth sledding if he still wants to be your 'special beau,'" I said. "He's been eating his heart out trying to figure you out, Cece."

"That will be tough sledding," laughed Peter.

"Why?" asked Cecily.

"It'll be tough sledding because there's no snow," joked Peter.

"Be serious, Peter," said Felicity with a rebuke.

"Just kidding," said Peter. Secretly he was glad that Felicity wasn't interested in Willy being her boyfriend. "Go on," he said with a smile.

"It's not a bad idea, Cece. I think you should let Willy know you like him," said the Story Girl.

"Oh, I can't do that. I'm too shy for—"

"Oh, no, you don't. This is no time for not telling the truth. That's just silly girl pride," I said. Everyone agreed.

"And I'm just the one to set Willy wise," said Peter, who was Willy's special friend.

"Maybe Aunt Janet will have something to say about her youngest having a boyfriend," said Felix wisely. "I mean, Cecily is just twelve."

"I think Mother won't mind if they're just friends," said Felicity. "But no smooching behind the schoolhouse."

"Don't worry about that," Cecily said, joining her as they left the school yard.

We all screamed with laughter. Cecily was so far from that, it was seriously funny. It was great to have things back to normal. Now we could be sarcastic with each other and have our fun. As I watched Felicity and Cecily leave the orchard with their arms around each other, I knew it wouldn't be long till they'd be scrapping together again, just like loving sisters. How strange that our quiet little sister had boys fighting over her and trying to win her heart. I guess it just proves that boys are more interested in sweetness than just a pretty face. Our smallest cousin had both. What a girl!

Aunt Una's Story

When we went into the garden, I saw an old stone bench in one corner, arched over by a couple of pear trees. The bench was all grown about with grass and violets, and a bent old man, with long, snow-white hair and beautiful sad blue eyes, was sitting on it.

Chapter Seven

elicity, Cecily, Dan, Felix, Sara Ray, and I were sitting on the mossy stones in Uncle Roger's hill pasture. We often sat there to listen to one of the Story Girl's stories, usually in the morning after we finished our chores. But it was evening now, and the valley beneath us was brimming with the glow of the approaching evening twilight. Behind us two tall, shapely spruce trees rose up against the sunset, and the first evening star looked down.

We sat on a little strip of emerald grassland, and before us was a sloping meadow all white with daisies. We were waiting for Peter and the Story Girl. Peter had gone to Markdale after dinner to spend the afternoon with his reunited parents because it was his birthday. He had told us he was going to confess to his father that he was a Presbyterian. We were anxious to know what his father had to say about it.

The Story Girl had gone that morning with Miss Reade to visit Miss Reade's home near Charlottetown.

We expected to see her coming home soon over the fields. But the first one to come up the hill was Peter.

"Hasn't Peter gotten tall?" said Cecily.

"Peter is growing to be a very fine-looking boy," said Felicity.

"I notice that you think he is fine now that his father is respectable and no longer a drunk," commented Dan. Felicity's pride had kept her from acknowledging Peter's good points before, though we could see that she was attracted to him. Now he was more attractive to her—an eligible young man for her to admire.

"I think he is more handsome now because he is free from care and responsibility," answered Felicity, defending her feelings for him.

"How did it go, Peter?" yelled Dan as soon as Peter was within earshot.

"Everything is all right," he responded happily. "I told Father as soon as I got home. I said, 'Dad, there's something I've got to tell you. While you were gone, I joined the Presbyterian church. It's not that I think it's any better than the Methodist, but my friends all went there, and Markdale Methodist is a long way from the King farm.' He said, 'Well, that's all right, Son. I'm just glad you joined a church. What brought that about?'

"I told him about the Judgment Day and how scared we were. And then I told him about the time

I nearly died when I had the measles. I said that I thought I needed to do something about my soul, in case I died.

"Father looked concerned when he heard about the measles, and said he was glad that I had taken the right step toward becoming a Christian. Then he said he didn't mind if I went to the Presbyterian church. He said what matters is that I want to live a godly life and go to church.

"I told him I was so happy about him being converted that I now wanted to go to the Methodist church with him and Mother. He was really pleased, and Mother had tears in her eyes. It's just like a dream come true to have him home and live a good Christian life. We had such a wonderful time together that I didn't even want to leave. He told me that I must do what is right. I tell you, Father is a Christian all right."

I spoke up then and told about Felix and I meeting up with them in the hardware store in Carlisle. "We just couldn't believe it was your father," I said. "They were like newlyweds and looked so handsome together."

"That's wonderful, Peter," said Felicity, with stars in her eyes. "I guess your mind can be at rest now. You can go to school and get a good education for—for later in life," she stammered. We knew she was thinking of her future, maybe with Peter.

Peter rolled his eyes at us, and we all laughed. Felicity did have some good points, and we had seen some real changes in her. We all knew that her friendship with Peter would be a good thing. He had such a fun sense of humor and was so stable. All of us remembered the great sermon he had preached at the Pulpit Stone. We had always thought he would make a great preacher. Perhaps even that was possible.

"Here comes the Story Girl," cried Cecily eagerly. "Now we'll hear all about Beautiful Alice's home."

The minute the Story Girl arrived, she was bombarded with eager questions. "Miss Reade's home is a dream of a place," she told them. "The house is covered with ivy, and there is a delightful old garden—with the sweetest little story connected to it. I saw the hero of the story too."

"Where was the heroine?" asked Cecily.

"She is dead."

"Oh, of course, she'd have to die," said Dan in disgust. "I'd like a story sometime where the people live."

"I've told you heaps of stories where people lived," retorted the Story Girl. "If this heroine hadn't died, there wouldn't have been any story. She was Miss Reade's aunt, and her name was Una. I believe she must have been just like Miss Reade herself. Miss Reade told me all about her.

"When we went into the garden, I saw an old stone bench in one corner, arched over by a couple of pear trees. The bench was all grown about with grass and violets, and a bent old man, with long, snow-white hair and beautiful sad blue eyes, was sitting on it. He seemed very lonely and sorrowful. I wondered why Miss Reade didn't speak to him. But she never let on that she saw him and took me away to another part of the garden.

"After a while he got up and went away. Then Miss Reade said, 'Come over to Aunt Una's seat, and I will tell you about her and her lover—the man who has just gone out.'"

"'Oh, isn't he too old for a lover?' I asked.

"Beautiful Alice laughed and said it had been forty years since he had been her aunt Una's lover. He had been a tall, handsome young man then, and her aunt Una was a beautiful girl of nineteen.

"We went over and sat down, and Miss Reade told me all about her. She said that when she was a child, she had heard a great deal about her aunt Una—she seemed to be the kind of person that people don't soon forget, whose personality seems to linger long after they have passed away.

"Miss Reade's aunt Una had a personality that was very uncommon. And she was beautiful, too, with white skin and night-black eyes and hair. Miss Reade said she had a moonlight beauty. Aunt Una kept a kind of diary, and Miss Reade's mother used to read parts of it to Miss Reade. She wrote verses in it, and they were lovely. She wrote descriptions of the old garden, which she loved very much.

"Miss Reade said that everything in the garden plot, or shrub, or tree, recalled to her mind some phrase or verse of her aunt Una's. The whole place seemed full of her, and her memory graced the walks like a faint, sweet perfume.

"Una had, as I've told you, a true love, and they were to have been married on her twentieth birthday. Her wedding dress was to have been a gown of white brocade with purple violets in it. But a short while before her wedding day, Una took ill with fever. On her birthday, she was buried instead of being married.

"Her beloved has been faithful to her through the years and has never married. Every June, on her birthday, he comes to the old garden and sits for a long time in silence on the bench where he used to woo her on moonlit nights long ago.

"Miss Reade says she always loves to see him sitting there because it gives her such a deep and lasting sense of the beauty, and strength of love, which can outlive time and death. And sometimes, she says, it gives her a little eerie feeling too. It is almost as if her aunt Una were really sitting there beside him, though she has been in her grave for forty years."

"It would be real romantic to die young and have your lover make a trip to your garden every year," reflected Sara Ray.

"It would be more comfortable to go on living and get married to him," said Felicity. "Mother says all those sentimental ideas are silly, and I expect they are. It's a wonder that Beautiful Alice doesn't have a boyfriend herself. She is so pretty and ladylike."

"The Carlisle fellows all say she is too stuck up," said Dan.

"There's nobody in Carlisle half good enough for her," cried the Story Girl, "except—except . . ."

"Except who?" asked Felix.

"Never mind," said the Story Girl mysteriously.

"Come on, Sara. You've been hinting at a lot of things. Does she have a boyfriend already?" asked Sara Ray. "Just tell us that."

"Well, I'll just say that she has a 'special interest' in someone."

"Does that someone have a 'special interest' in her?" asked Felix. He was always interested in romantic stories. I think he missed our mother and liked to hear stories with happy endings.

"Maybe," said the Story Girl vaguely.

"Do we know him?" asked Cecily eagerly.

"That would be a 'yes,'" responded Sara. "You do know him, but you'd never guess in a hundred years. He is most unlikely as a boyfriend for Miss Reade."

"Do you like him, Sara?" asked Felicity.

"Oh yes, very much."

"Ohhhhh, I have an idea," enthused Cecily. "Will you tell me if I guess right?"

"No, Cecily. I have been asked not to tell. I have sworn upon my honor. If it ever comes about, I will tell you if you were right."

Aunt Olivia's Wedding

Aunt Olivia was married at five o'clock
in the orchard under her large apple tree.
It was a pretty scene. The air was full of
the perfume of apple blossoms, and the
bees blundered foolishly and delightfully
from one bloom to another.

Chapter Eight

What a delightful, old-fashioned, wholesome excitement there was about Aunt Olivia's wedding. We didn't go to school for two days before the event, so that we could do chores and run errands. The cooking, decorating, and arranging that went on for those two days was truly amazing. Felicity was so happy over it all that she didn't even quarrel with Dan. She nearly did, though, when he told her the governor's wife was coming to the wedding. He couldn't resist teasing her about the cinnamon toast she had made with tooth powder when the governor's wife had visited us.

"I'm sure everyone makes a mistake now and then," she observed. "Just keep quiet, Dan, or I'll tell some things you might not like others to hear," she warned.

"I suppose none of us except the Story Girl will get to eat at the head table," said Felix, rather gloomily.

"Never mind," comforted Felicity. "There's a whole turkey to be kept for us, and a bucket full of

97

ice cream. Cecily and I are going to wait on the tables, and we'll put away a little of everything that's extra nice for our supper."

"I do so want to have my supper with you," sighed Sara Ray, "but I suppose Ma will drag me with her wherever she goes. She won't trust me out of her sight a minute for the whole evening—I know she won't."

"I'll get Aunt Olivia to ask her to let you have your supper with us," said Cecily. "She can't refuse the bride's request."

"You don't know all Ma can do," returned Sara darkly. "No, I'll just have to eat my supper with her. But I suppose I should be very thankful that I'm coming to the wedding at all. And Ma did get me a new white dress for it. Still, I'm scared something will happen to prevent me from going to it."

Monday evening was cloudy and windy, and by Tuesday the rain came. It was quite a downpour. What if it kept raining on Wednesday—the day of the wedding? Aunt Olivia couldn't be married in the orchard then. That would be an awful shame since the apple tree that was named for Aunt Olivia had kept all its blossoms, while most of the others had faded. Her tree had been unusually late in blooming that year, just as though it had timed its blooming on purpose. It was a sight to see. Never had a bride had a more beautiful canopy. But, oh, the rain! What would we do if it kept pouring on Wednesday?

To our great delight and in answer to our prayers, the rain cleared up beautifully Tuesday evening. The sun, before setting, poured a flood of wonderful sunshine over the whole diamond-dripping world and promised to shine beautifully for the wedding day. Uncle Alec drove off through the drips to bring the bridegroom and best man home.

Dan was full of a wild idea that we should all meet them at the gate with cowbells and tin pans, as was the old custom called "shivaree." Peter sided with him, but the rest of us voted him down.

"Do you want Dr. Seton to think his new nieces and nephews are uncivilized?" asked Felicity severely. "A nice opinion he'd have of our manners!"

"Well, it's the only chance we'll have to shivaree them," grumbled Dan. "Aunt Olivia won't mind. *She* can take a joke."

"Ma would have a fit if you did such a thing," warned Felicity. "Dr. Seton lives in Halifax, and they *never* shivaree people there. He would think it very vulgar."

"Then he should have stayed in Halifax and gotten married there," retorted Dan in a sulk.

We were very curious to see our uncle-to-be. When Uncle Alec took him into the parlor, we all crowded into the dark corner behind the stairs to peep at him. Then we ran outside to the dairy and discussed him.

"He's bald," said Cecily with disappointment.

"And rather short and stout," said Felicity.

"He's forty, if he's a day," said Dan.

"Never mind," cried the Story Girl loyally. "Aunt Olivia loves him with all her heart."

"And more than that, he's got lots of money," added Felicity.

"Well, he may be all right," said Peter, "but it's my opinion that your aunt Olivia could have found someone just as good on the island."

"Your opinion doesn't matter very much to *our* family," said Felicity proudly.

But when we got to know Dr. Seton early the next morning, we liked him a lot and voted him a great fellow. All of us were out in the orchard while the dew was still on the blossoms. It was our job to gather as many cherry and peach blossoms as we could. We had large buckets that we had to fill. They had to be placed at the ends of each row of the chairs we had borrowed from the church for the wedding. It was a huge job and seemed overwhelming to us.

Aunt Janet had said the blossoms needed to be picked and placed in water before breakfast so they wouldn't wilt. We were all hungry and grumpy from getting up early.

"Why isn't it enough just to have the canopy of apple blossoms?" grumped Felix. "Seems that ought to be enough for any bride."

"Just get picking and fill your buckets," advised Felicity. "We have lots to do after this is done. Be thankful that you're not a girl and have to fix the food too," she said.

Just then we heard the gate to the orchard creak open. Uncle Robert appeared, dressed in his work clothes. He smiled a good morning and fell right in, helping us just as if he were one of us.

"I thought you all could use a little help," he said.

"Glad to have you, Uncle Robert. We have a ton of work to do," I said.

"I thought so," was his reply. Before we knew it, we were filling our buckets without even realizing that it was work we were doing. He began telling story after story, mostly about weddings, and had us laughing our heads off.

He told one story about a groom who was so nervous that he forgot his pants and started down the aisle without them. The bride turned her back to him modestly, grabbed her veil, and threw it around him. Then they went right on down the aisle. Later, when asked why she didn't let him go back and get his pants, she had a good reason. "I wasn't about to give him a chance to run away once I got him to the altar," she said.

Then he told another story about a bride who was so fat that they had to take the doors off the church to get her down the aisle. When someone asked the groom if he didn't mind her being so heavy, he had a good answer too. "I figger anyone as big as that must be a good cook. Also, she won't be wanting to run off and leave me. She couldn't fit in another man's buggy."

Another one was about a groom who fainted. To bring him around, the best man threw a bucket of water all over him. He sat up spluttering and promptly threw up all over his wedding clothes. Uncle Robert was the only doctor in the church, so they asked him what to do. He said he told the groom not to look at his bride during the wedding. She was making him too nervous. Sure enough he turned so he couldn't see her, and they got married. Uncle Robert said the bride must not have been too hard-looking for him because they've now been married eight years and have three children.

He told another one about being called to a hotel after a wedding. It seemed the groom had tried to carry his hefty bride across the threshold at the hotel and had ruptured a disc in his back. They had to carry the groom out to Uncle Robert's office, where he tried to help him with his pain. The couple had to postpone their honeymoon for a month. When they came home from their honeymoon, the groom didn't even try to carry her over the threshold again.

We were howling with laughter when we heard the orchard gate creak again. Aunt Olivia was coming to see what was going on in the orchard. The Story Girl went running toward her and stopped her from coming into the orchard. It was an old tradition that the bride and groom shouldn't see each other on their wedding day before the ceremony.

Aunt Olivia pooh-poohed the old idea that it was bad luck for the groom to see the bride before the wedding. She said that didn't matter to them. But she did leave before seeing him. She said she had a lot to do and would let us enjoy getting to know Robert.

There was no doubt about it. We loved our new uncle. The only sad thing was that they would live so far away from us. We couldn't wait to get to Halifax and meet all the brides and grooms he had told us about. While we were finishing the decorating, Peter said he guessed Miss Olivia hadn't made too much of a mistake not marrying someone from our island. The Story Girl said that several men had asked Aunt Olivia to marry them, but she had waited until she knew she had the right one.

The girls didn't have much time to discuss him with us. As soon as we finished gathering the blossoms and fixing them, the girls took off for the kitchen to help prepare the food. They were all running here and there like chickens with their heads cut off. Felicity bossed everyone around as though she were the queen. But soon things were in place and finished.

"I have a note from Sara Ray," said Cecily. "Judy Pineau brought it up when she brought the salad Mrs. Ray made for the wedding supper. Let me read it to you.

"'Dearest Cecily: A dreadful misfortune has happened to me. Last night I went with Judy to get the cows, and we found a wasps' nest in a spruce bush. Judy thought it was an *old* one, and she poked it with a stick. We quickly found that it was a *new* one—full of wasps. They all flew out and stung us on the face and hands. My face is so swollen that I can hardly see out of one eye. The suffering was awful, but I was more scared that Ma wouldn't take me to the wedding.

"'But she says I can go and *I'm going*. I know that I am a hard-looking sight, but it isn't anything catching. I am writing this so you won't get a shock when you see me. Isn't it so strange to think your dear aunt Olivia is going away? How you will miss her! But your loss will be her gain.

"'Your loving chum, Sara Ray.'"

"That poor child," said the Story Girl.

"Well, all I hope is that strangers won't think

she is one of the family." remarked Felicity in a disgusted voice.

Aunt Olivia was married at five o'clock in the orchard under her large apple tree. It was a pretty scene. The air was full of the perfume of apple blossoms, and the bees blundered foolishly and delightfully from one bloom to another. It was as though the bees were half drunk with perfume.

The old orchard was full of smiling guests in wedding garments. Aunt Olivia was beautiful under the frost of her bridal veil. The Story Girl wore an unusually long white dress of beautiful lace. She had her brown curls arranged in a shining coil and looked so tall and grown-up that we hardly recognized her.

After the ceremony—during which Sara Ray cried the whole time—there was a royal wedding supper. Sara Ray was permitted to eat her share of the feast with us.

"I'm glad I was stung by the wasps after all," she said delightedly. "If I hadn't been, Ma would never have let me eat with you. She just got tired of explaining to people what was wrong with my face. So she was glad to be rid of me. I know I look awful, but, oh, wasn't the bride a dream?"

We missed the Story Girl, who, of course, had to have her supper at the bridal table with the rest of the wedding party. But we were a hilarious little crew, and the girls kept their promise to save tidbits for us. By the time the last table was cleared away, Aunt Olivia and our new uncle were ready to go. There were lots of tears as they said their good-bye.

When they drove away into the moonlit night, Dan and Peter ran after them down the lane with bells and pans. Felicity was mortified, but Aunt Olivia and Uncle Robert took it well and waved their hands back to us, laughing as they rode away.

"They're so happy they wouldn't mind if there was an earthquake," said Felix grinning.

"It's been splendid, and everything went off well," sighed Cecily. "But, oh, it's going to be lonesome without Aunt Olivia. I just believe I'll cry all night."

"You're bone tired—that's what's the matter with you," said Dan, returning from the shivaree of the wedding couple. "You girls have worked like slaves today."

"Tomorrow will be even harder," complained Felicity. "Everything will have to be cleaned up and put away. It will take us hours of work," she sighed.

The next day, Peg Bowen paid us a call, knowing that she would get a good feast of leftovers.

"Well, I've had all I can eat," she said, when she had finished and brought out her pipe. "And that doesn't happen to me every day. There ain't been as much marryin' as there used to be. Half the time couples just sneak off to the minister, as if they're ashamed of it. Then they git married without any wedding supper at all. That ain't the King way though. You folks always do it up right.

"And so Olivia's got herself a man," she continued. "And I hear tell he's got money. She weren't in any hurry, so she got herself a good 'un."

"Why don't you get married yourself, Peg?" asked Uncle Roger teasingly. We held our breath at his daring to question her.

"Because I'm not easy to please," she retorted, laughing.

She left in high, good humor. Meeting Sara Ray on the doorstep, she stopped and asked her what was the matter with her face.

"Wasps," answered Sara with a smile. "I know I look terrible but I can't help it."

"Them wasp stings will go away soon," said Peg Bowen. "And one of these days you'll be a 'purty' girl."

We all laughed at her. But in a few days the stings and welts were gone. Life had improved for Sara Ray. She actually looked quite pretty as she gave her recitation at the school conference.

Even though life changed over the summer since Aunt Olivia was gone, we cousins enjoyed the Golden Road each day—together.

Lucy Maud Montgomery
1908

Lucy Maud Montgomery
1874-1942

Anne of Green Gables was the very first book that Lucy Maud Montgomery published. In all, she wrote twenty-five books.

Lucy Maud Montgomery was born on Prince Edward Island. Her family called her Maud. Before she was two years old, her mother died and she was sent to live with her mother's parents on their farm on the Island. Her grandparents were elderly and very strict. Maud lived with them for a long time.

When she was seven, her father remarried. He moved far out west to Saskatchewan, Canada, with his new wife. At age seventeen, she went to live with them, but she did not get along with her stepmother. So she returned to her grandparents.

She attended college and studied to become a teacher—just like Anne in the Avonlea series. When her grandfather died, Maud went home to be with her grandmother. Living there in the quiet of Prince Edward Island, she had plenty of time to write. It was during this time that she wrote her first book, *Anne of Green Gables*. When the book was finally accepted, it was published soon after. It was an immediate hit, and Maud began to get thousands of letters asking for more stories about Anne. She wrote *Anne of Avonlea, Chronicles of Avonlea, Anne of the Island, Anne of Windy Poplars, Anne's House of Dreams, Rainbow Valley, Anne of Ingleside,* and *Rilla of Ingleside*. She also wrote *The Story Girl* and *The Golden Road*.

When Maud was thirty-seven years old, Ewan Macdonald, the minister of the local Presbyterian Church in Canvendish, proposed marriage to her. Maud accepted and they were married. Later on they moved to Ontario where two sons, Chester and Stewart, were born to the couple.

Maud never went back to Prince Edward Island to live again. But when she died in 1942, she was buried on the Island, near the house known as Green Gables.

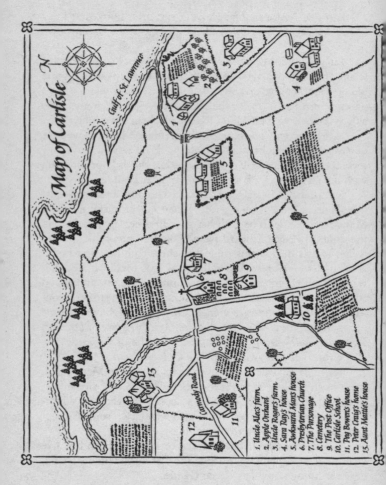

Map of Carlisle

N

Gulf of St. Lawrence

Carmody Road

1. Uncle Alec's farm.
2. Apple Orchard
3. Uncle Roger's farm.
4. Sara Ray's house
5. Awkward Man's house
6. Presbyterian Church
7. The Parsonage
8. Cemetery
9. The Post Office
10. Carlisle School
11. Peg Bowen's house
12. Peter Craig's home
13. Aunt Mattie's house

Enjoy heartwarming stories of childhood antics, tall-tales, and legends of a time long past with *The Story Girl*™ series

Written by L.M. Montgomery,
Adapted by Barbara Davoll

Available now at your local bookstore!

zonder**kidz**

zonder**kidz**.

We want to hear from you. Please send your comments
about this book to us in care of zreview@zondervan.com. Thank you.

Grand Rapids, MI 49530
www.zonderkidz.com